BY ALAN DURANT

ILLUSTRATED BY SUE MASON

Librarian Reviewer
Marci Peschke
Librarian, Dallas Independent School District
MA Education Reading Specialist, Stephen F. Austin State University
Learning Resources Endorsement, Texas Women's University

Reading Consultant
Sherry Klehr
Elementary/Middle School Educator, Edina Public Schools, MN
MA in Education, University of Minnesota

STONE ARCH BOOKS
Minneapolis San Diego

First published in the United States in 2008
by Stone Arch Books, A Capstone Imprint
151 Good Counsel Drive, P.O. Box 669,
Mankato, Minnesota 56002
www.capstonepub.com

Published by arrangement with
Barrington Stoke Ltd, Edinburgh.

Library of Congress Cataloging-in-Publication Data
Durant, Alan, 1958–
    [Game Boy Reloaded.]
    Gamer: Next Level / by Alan Durant; illustrated by Sue Mason.
    p. cm. — (Pathway Books)
    Originally published under title: Game Boy Reloaded.
    Summary: Mia is shocked when a video game cartridge found in a canal
draws both her and her brother into a game experience that is very real--and
very dangerous.
    ISBN-13: 978-1-59889-873-6 (library binding)
    ISBN-10: 1-59889-873-6 (library binding)
    ISBN-13: 978-1-59889-909-2 (paperback)
    ISBN-10: 1-59889-909-0 (paperback)
    [1. Video games—Fiction. 2. Brothers and sisters—Fiction. 3. Science
fiction.] I. Mason, Sue, ill. II. Title.
PZ7.D9317Gan 2008
[Fic]—dc22   2007006621

Art Director: Heather Kindseth
Graphic Designer: Brann Garvey

Printed in the United States of America in Stevens Point, Wisconsin.
082010
005926R

TABLE OF CONTENTS

CHAPTER 1

THE MYSTERY GAME

"Get away from there, Zak!"
Mia shouted.

Mia often shouted at Zak. He was her
little brother, and he was a pest. He was
always doing things he shouldn't. Just
now he was throwing stones into the
river. That was okay, but he was standing
too close to the water. He might fall in,
and then they'd both be in trouble.

Mom had told Mia to look after Zak.

"He's old enough to look after himself," Mia had grumbled.

Mom didn't think so. So here Mia was, looking after her little brother once again. She wanted to be in her room, playing *Planet Quest* on her Z Box video game player. It wasn't fair.

"Zak, don't be silly! Get away from there!" Mia shouted again.

Zak didn't listen. He never did. Mia marched up to him.

"Look, Mia," Zak said. He pointed at something floating in the water. "Look!"

She was too mad to look. "It's just a piece of trash," she said while pulling Zak back. The river was full of trash. "Now get away. It's all muddy here."

But Zak wouldn't come. "No, look," he said again. "It looks like a Z Box game. Over there, in the water."

This time Mia did look. She loved her Z Box. Zak also loved the Z Box, but she never let him play it. He took it sometimes when she wasn't around, and he never put it back. It drove her crazy.

"I'm going to get it," Zak said.

"No, stay here," said Mia. "You'll only get wet. I'll try."

Mia found a long stick. She reached out into the water to pull the floating thing in. She thought it would be hard, but it was easy. The thing seemed to move toward her on its own. It was a small, gray box. Zak was right. It was a Z Box game!

Mia was excited as she picked the game out of the water. Zak was excited, too. He ran over. "Let's see, let's see!" he kept shouting.

Mia held it away from him. She shook the water off. "It's mine," she said.

"I saw it first!" he complained.

"But I got it out," Mia said.

They looked at the game together. It had no picture or name on it. There was a line of print. Mia rubbed the game dry on her shorts.

"Warning! This experience may seriously damage your health," she read aloud. She frowned. "Weird," she said.

"Cool," said Zak. "I wonder what game it is."

Mia gave a shrug. "I don't think it'll work anyway," she said. "The water has probably ruined it."

"Let's try it," said Zak.

"I will," said Mia, "as soon as we get home."

She put the game in her pocket.

Suddenly Zak put his hand on Mia's arm. "Somebody's watching us," he whispered with a shiver. "Look on the bridge."

Mia gave a sigh. Zak was always imagining things. When she looked, she saw that Zak was right. There was a man standing on the bridge over the river.

He was staring at them.

The man looked strange. He was bald, except for a small cone of white hair on top of his head. He wore thick glasses that made his eyes look huge. His eyes had an odd gleam to them, too. He smiled at Mia, showing a row of teeth with silver caps.

Now Mia shivered too. "Let's go," she said. She grabbed Zak's hand, and they ran away.

CHAPTER 2

STARTING THE GAME

Mia wanted to try out the game as soon as she got home. She went to her room and took her Z Box down from the shelf. She loaded the new game. Would it work after it had gotten wet? She didn't get the chance to find out. Just as she was about to turn on her Z Box, Mia's mom called her.

Mia dropped the Z Box on her bed and went downstairs.

Half an hour later, Mia could finally go back upstairs. Her mom had wanted to check her spelling homework, and then Mia had to set the table for lunch. When she got back to her room, Mia was angry to see that the Z Box and her new game were gone.

"Zak!" she yelled. "Just wait until I get my hands on him! That little pest!"

Mia stomped into Zak's room. Yes, the Z Box was there all right, just as she guessed. It was lying on Zak's bed. There was no sign at all of her little brother. He had been playing the game. The Z Box was still on and it felt warm.

Mia looked at the screen. There was an underwater scene with seaweed and fish. Well, at least the game worked. That was good.

Mia sat down on Zak's bed and pushed her thumbs down on the controls. There was no little person to move around. In this game, everything was happening to you, the player. She'd played plenty of games like that before.

She moved her left thumb over the direction controls and pressed the A button. She moved in and out of the plants. Should she catch or dodge the fish that came onto the screen now and then? She decided to play safe and dodge them for the moment.

Mia moved faster as she got used to the game. Now she was racing across the seafloor. She jumped over any rocks that blocked her way. It was easy and fun. There weren't any real dangers. That's how it seemed anyway.

Then she saw the jellyfish.

They were falling through the water like purple parachutes. Mia knew she had to dodge them. Jellyfish stung. If she bumped into one of them, they would take away some of her power. They might hurt her. She didn't know how poisonous the jellyfish were. She didn't want to find out.

She waited until the first group of jellyfish had dropped and vanished. Then she ran as fast as she could. She froze when the next group fell, and then dodged them too. One nearly got her, but she took a step back just in time.

At last, she was past the jellyfish. She saw in the sea ahead of her some kind of wreck. Maybe it was an old ship full of treasure. That would be cool.

Mia was enjoying the game now.
She could feel the cold water against her
skin. She could taste its saltiness. Then
she saw a boy! He was standing on the
old ship, waving at her. She stopped,
amazed and confused.

It was Zak, and behind him was a
giant octopus! Its tentacles were reaching
out toward Zak.

Mia tried to shout a warning, but her
cry was lost in bubbles.

The tentacles closed around Zak.

There was nothing Mia could do.

An instant later, Zak and the octopus
vanished into the wreck.

CHAPTER 3

RACING THE SHARK

Mia was in shock. She had just seen her little brother inside the game she was playing. Then she saw him grabbed by a giant octopus.

Most shocking of all, Mia knew that she wasn't lying on Zak's bed playing her Z Box anymore. Now she was part of the game. She was playing it from the inside! She was really under the sea! The wreck was really there in front of her.

Mia shut her eyes and shook her head, but nothing changed. She was still underwater. Only this wasn't like being underwater in real life. She could breathe like a fish. She could walk along the bottom of the sea, too.

Somehow, she and Zak had been sucked into the game. It was incredible. No wonder the game had a warning!

Mia didn't understand what had happened. Still, she knew what she had to do next. She had to get inside the wreck and rescue her little brother. She'd wasted too much time already. The octopus could have crushed him by now.

Mia ran until she got to the wreck. She looked for a door or a place to enter. Zak and the octopus had gotten in, so there had to be a way.

At last she saw an opening. It was a jagged hole in the ship's side. If she jumped up and kicked her legs, she should be able to swim through.

Something moved in the water near her. She looked around quickly and gasped. It was a shark, a great white shark with a mouth full of huge teeth. It was heading for her!

There was no time to lose. Mia jumped and kicked hard and fast. She pushed up through the water with her arms. Would she reach the hole before the shark reached her?

She could see the shark out of the corner of her eye. It was racing toward her with its fin cutting through the water and its mouth open ready to snap.

Mia swam harder, stronger, and kicked even faster.

She was at the hole. Her head was through. Now her body was through. The shark was right behind her.

One last kick! Mia dragged her legs up, and she was through. She had made it into the ship!

Everything went black.

CHAPTER 4

THE TREASURE CHEST

Mia gave a big sigh of relief. She had made it, but just barely. That had been too close.

When Mia looked down, she saw that the bottoms of her shoes were torn to shreds. If she'd been even a little bit slower, the shark would have gotten her! She'd have had to go back to the start of the game. Then how would she ever have found Zak?

Mia looked around. If this was a game, then she must be on the next level. There was no sign of Zak, so Mia swam through another hole up to the next deck.

There wasn't much on this deck either, except some old ropes and a few rusty cannons. There was still no sign of Zak. Mia was going to keep swimming upward, but changed her mind. There were some small gold coins floating in the water around the deck. She thought she should collect them. Players often collected things in Z Box games. The coins might give her power or energy.

Mia took a step to the left and grabbed a coin. She was surprised at how light it felt. The coin was as light as a feather.

She put the first coin in her pocket and moved on. She collected a second coin and a third, fourth, and fifth. As she reached to grab more coins, the wooden floor started cracking.

"Ow!" she cried. Her left foot went straight through the floor. Now the board under her right foot started to creak and crack. She pulled out her left foot and stepped away quickly. Looking at the floor she could see that the wood was rotten and split in lots of places. It wasn't safe to walk across.

Her leg hurt. No wonder! There was a big splinter of wood in it. Mia had gotten splinters before, but never one this big. She had to get it out. She grabbed the loose end of the splinter, shut her eyes, and yanked.

"Ah!" Mia screamed. The splinter came out, and there wasn't even a mark on her skin.

Weird, she thought. Then again, this was a weird game.

She decided not to pick up any more coins. Instead she swam up again.

The next deck up was empty, too. No, hold on a minute. In the corner was some kind of box. She went closer, stepping carefully on the creaky boards.

It wasn't a box. It was a treasure chest! Mia saw something else, too. In front of the chest was a small blue shoe. It was Zak's. He had been here! She was on the right track. Zak wasn't there now. Did the octopus get him or had Zak gotten away?

Mia needed to find out. But how? There didn't seem to be any way out from this deck of the ship.

Mia walked around the deck carefully. She was looking for a hidden door or a way to escape. No, there wasn't one. It had to be the chest then. The answer must be in there. She went toward it.

Mia was almost in front of the chest when something made her stop and look down. The boards on the floor didn't look right. They were cracked, but the cracks had clean smooth edges, and they made a perfect square. Mia bent down to look.

She rested her hand on the wooden square and pushed softly. Whomp! The wood dropped open. It was a trapdoor! Mia almost fell, but she stopped herself just in time.

Mia moved back. One of the coins she had picked up fell out of her pocket and into the hole. She watched it spin through the dark, down and down, until it vanished. She listened, but didn't hear the coin land. She shivered. That could have been her.

Mia stepped around the hole in the floor with great care. Now she was in front of the chest. She touched it. It felt solid. She tried to lift the lid, but she couldn't make it move. There was no key, not even any lock, just a tiny slot in the front of the chest.

Mia put her eye against the slot, but all she could see was darkness. She ran her hand over the chest. Maybe there was a secret button that might open the lid! She couldn't find one.

Mia was getting frustrated. She had gotten this far, but now she was stuck. Zak had gotten to the next level, so she should've been able to. She was a much better Z Box player than he was, the little pest. Think, Mia, she said to herself. If you were at the controls now, how would you solve this problem?

She looked again at the tiny slot in the chest, and then she knew. This wasn't a treasure chest. It was a giant bank! Mia took one of the coins out of her pocket and slipped it into the slot in the chest. It was a perfect fit. The chest's lid quickly flew open.

Mia climbed in. The lid slammed shut behind her.

CHAPTER 5

CHOOSING A PATH

Mia was on an island. Behind her was the sea and in front of her was an old castle. That must be where she had to go on this level, she thought. Right in front of her were three paths. She had to choose which one to take. Mia sat down on a rock to think.

Mia put her hand in her pocket. She wanted to see if the gold coins were still there in this new level. She only had two left. Three were gone.

One of the coins had dropped out when she nearly fell through the trapdoor. She had used one to open the chest. What about the third coin?

Mia remembered the splinter and how her skin had suddenly gotten better. She must have used up a coin then. The coins were like magic. Well, it was good that she still had two left for this new level. She would need them.

Mia looked at the three paths. Which one went to the castle? The one on the left headed into the woods. The one on the right went down to the sea. To get to the castle she had to go up, not down. The middle one looked the best. Yes, she'd take the middle path.

Mia had wasted a lot of time already, so she ran down the path. She kept looking out for any dangers.

She nearly ran into a small monkey that jumped down in front of her. An instant later, two more jumped down. They looked friendly. In this game, though, you had to be ready for anything.

Mia moved forward slowly. There were lots more monkeys now, but they didn't show any interest in her. They reminded her of Zak, except much nicer.

Mia was so busy staring at the monkeys that she didn't see the circle of rope on the ground. She stepped into it. The rope went tight around her ankle.

"Agh!" she yelled. The rope yanked her ankle and then the rest of her body up through the air! She was hanging upside down from a tree. That wasn't the worst thing. The path had come to a dead end. Now she was dangling over the edge of a cliff!

"Help!" she cried, but there was no point. Who could hear her? For once she wished that Zak was around. The rope jerked and Mia twisted around to look up. The branch the rope was tied to was breaking. Soon it would snap and she would fall onto the rocks far below.

Mia tried to swing herself to the cliff edge and grip onto something. All she did was jiggle another coin out of her pocket. It fell past her.

"No!" she shouted. "No, no, no!"

Suddenly she felt a tug on her ankle. She was being pulled up toward the tree.

"Hey," she shouted. What on earth was going on now?

As soon as she was close, Mia reached out and grabbed a thick branch. It was hard work, but she dragged herself onto the branch. She pulled herself along the branch until at last she was safely above the path again. Suddenly, the rope vanished. She took a deep breath. That's it, she thought, another coin gone. Only one more left.

Mia had chosen the wrong path. She should have known that the simple choice wouldn't be the right one. Nothing in this game was that easy.

Mia went back and tried another path. The forest path came to a dead end too. The path that went down to the sea had to be the right one, she thought.

The path went down and up, down and up, this way and that. Mia climbed over fallen trees and crawled through small tunnels. It was hard work. Her legs hurt by the time she could see the castle again. Normally, when she played her Z Box game all that hurt was her thumbs.

Mia stood still for a few moments and stared at the castle. It was huge. It had a drawbridge entrance and high walls. At the very top was a tower in the shape of a skull. A flag with a picture of a skull and crossbones on it flapped in the wind. This was a pirate castle!

Mia could see something else, too. There was someone in the tower. A tiny figure was leaning out of one of the windows of the skull tower and waving. Even from far away, Mia knew it was Zak! He looked like he was trapped in the tower.

"Zak!" Mia shouted. "Zak! Don't worry. I'm coming."

She ran along the path to the castle, crossed the drawbridge, and raced inside.

Everything went black.

CHAPTER 6

THE HALL OF SWORDS

A warning flashed in the darkness.

Beware! You have entered the Castle of Redbeard, the Pirate King. Your life is in danger. Many enter, but few leave. Do you dare continue?

Mia had to go on. She had no choice. Zak needed her, and she also wanted to find out how this game ended. She wasn't going to give up now.

Mia walked through a large hall and up a huge, stone staircase. There were pirate pictures on the walls. She felt as if they were watching her. The pictures gave Mia the creeps. Suddenly, she thought about the weird guy with the cone of white hair who'd been standing on the bridge. He had creeped her out too. She remembered with a shiver the way he'd stared and smiled. Did he have something to do with this game?

Mia walked on. Ahead of her was a dark hallway, lit by a few smoky candles. She gasped as she got closer. On each side of the hallway was a row of pirates. They all had swords and stood as still as statues. They held their swords up as if they were ready to strike.

If they were just statues, then Mia didn't need to worry. But they looked so real with their mean faces and their evil eyes.

Mia was close to the first pirate now. She waited a moment. She wanted to be sure it was safe to pass between the two rows of pirates. She took a small step forward then jumped back.

Whoosh!

All the pirates' swords chopped down together, then slowly lifted again. Mia had been right to wait. If she would have walked down the hallway she'd have been carved up like a turkey!

Mia tried again. She stepped forward and jumped back.

This time she counted the seconds while the swords were being lifted up. Nine seconds. That's how long she had to get to the end of the hallway. She had to run down the hallway while the pirates were lifting up their swords. Could she do it?

At the end of the hallway, beyond the pirates, she could see some stairs. Mia had to climb them to reach the top of the castle and get into the tower. That's where Zak was. She had no choice. She had to get to the stairs to rescue Zak.

Mia shut her eyes and took a deep breath. Come on, you can do it, she said to herself. She was the fastest runner in her school, so she should be okay. But this time she was running for her life.

Mia got herself into a good starting position. She put one leg a little in front of the other, bent her knees, and got her arms ready to pump. She was ready. She took a small step forward, then back.

Whoosh!

The swords chopped down again. Mia waited, ready. The moment the swords started to lift, she was off.

Run, Mia, run! she told herself.

Within seconds she was halfway to the end of the pirates. Her feet seemed to be flying. She was going to make it. Then disaster struck! She lost her balance and stumbled, falling to the floor. By the time she'd picked herself up, the swords were almost up above the pirates' heads. In an instant they'd chop down again.

Mia didn't have time to think. She ran faster than ever before. As she reached the last pirate, Mia saw his sword starting to come down. She threw herself forward, chest out, like an Olympic racer stretching for the finish line.

Whoosh!

Mia heard the swords chop down. She felt something brush the back of her head. Then she fell, panting and gasping.

Mia put her hand up to her head and shivered. She felt her scalp. The sword had cut away some of her hair. She almost didn't make it. But the important thing was that she'd reached the end of another level. How many more levels were there?

CHAPTER 7

PARROT ATTACK

Mia climbed the stairs. They were narrow and went around and around on their way upward. She was puffing by the time she reached the top.

Ahead of her was a doorway and beyond that the skull tower. There was a sword hanging next to the arch. It was about time she had a weapon, she thought. You never knew what to expect next in this game. Mia took the sword off the wall and stepped through the arch.

Now she could see the skull tower clearly. Was Zak still there? She called out his name. A few moments later she saw him waving from one of the skull's eye windows.

"Mia!" he shouted. "Mia, I'm trapped. I can't get out."

"It's okay, Zak!" Mia shouted back. "I'm coming to get you."

Suddenly Zak's hand shot up, pointing at something. "Look out, Mia!" he screamed.

Mia looked up. Something was flying at her. She dodged just in time and the thing passed by with an evil squawk. It looked like some kind of parrot. Mia had never heard of parrots attacking people.

Squawk, squawk!

Mia turned to see another parrot. It had evil red eyes, and its beak and claws looked very sharp. This was no Pretty Polly. This was a killer pirate parrot, and it was heading right at her! Mia swung her sword in the air.

Swish!

The parrot vanished. There were more, lots of them, preparing to attack.

Mia started to run toward the tower. She had to save Zak.

Another parrot swooped down and squawked. Mia swung the sword twice and the bird vanished. Normally, you'd have to actually strike the parrot with the sword. Mia was glad that in this game it was different. But how many more parrots were there?

Mia had gone the wrong way! She wasn't at the skull tower. In front of her was a wall and nothing else. She had to turn and go back. Mia tried a different way, running as fast as she could.

Two more parrots swooped at her, squawking.

Mia waved her sword and the first bird vanished. She waved again, but nothing happened! The second bird was almost on her now. She could see its mouth open as it got ready to rip its sharp beak into her. Mia threw her sword at the bird. The bird screeched and vanished. Mia gave a sigh. She was still alive, but now she didn't have a weapon.

"Mia, look out! Hurry!" Zak yelled.

Mia looked and gasped. A whole flock of parrots was getting ready to swoop.

She couldn't dodge all of them. She had to get to the tower before they got to her. Once again she was in a race for her life.

Mia ran toward the tower. This time, she went the right way.

Mia ran up the stairs to the tower door. She reached it just as the parrots dived at her. She rattled the iron door handle, pushed, rattled again. The door was stuck! She ducked as the first parrot swooped down at her, then pushed at the door as hard as she could. This time it swung open and she fell inside.

The door slammed shut behind her.

CHAPTER 8

THE PIRATE'S PUZZLE

"You made it, Mia, you made it!"
Zak threw his arms around his sister.
Mia held him tight until he could tell
her what had happened. Zak had been
sucked into the game like her. At first he
thought it was really cool, even when
the octopus had grabbed him. He had
wiggled free and escaped into the wreck.
It had been an exciting adventure, but
now he'd had enough.

"I don't want to play this game any more, Mia," Zak sobbed. "I want to go home."

Mia hugged her little brother. "It's okay, Zak," she said softly. "This must be the last level. We'll be home soon."

"But we're locked in," Zak said. "How can we get out?"

"Don't worry," said Mia. "We'll find a way. We have to."

Mia got up and went over to the door she had entered. It was shut tight and there was no handle on this side. She climbed into one of the windows and looked out. It was too high up to jump and the tower walls were too smooth to climb down.

Suddenly, there was a red flash and a ghostly figure floated in the air in front of them.

It was a pirate with a patch over one eye and the biggest and reddest beard that Mia had ever seen. Redbeard! Of course, it was Redbeard, the Pirate King, who owned this castle. Zak grabbed Mia's hand. She could tell he was terrified. Mia was pretty scared herself.

"Shiver me timbers!" Redbeard roared. As he spoke, the words flashed up on the walls around him. "You've made it through to the end. Well done. But it ain't quite over yet. No. There be one final test." Redbeard pointed to the floor and a puzzle with squares and letters flashed onto it.

"You're inside the skull, landlubbers, and now it's time to use your brains," he said. "Find the hidden message and you win. Be fast about it! You have one minute to complete the task." Redbeard pointed at the wall and a candle lit up. "When the candle burns out, the tower will fall. Good luck and farewell!"

Suddenly, there was another red flash and Redbeard disappeared. The candle started to burn down.

"Quick," said Mia. "We've got to solve this puzzle." She stared at the letters, then back at the candle. It was melting fast. She was terrible at word puzzles. She'd never been good at reading or spelling. That's why she had to do extra work at home with her Mom.

How could she possibly do this puzzle in time? The candle was almost half gone.

"Mia!" Zak shouted.

Mia stopped worrying about what to do. She looked down and saw Zak on the ground, moving the letters around. At first she thought that he was just being a pest as always.

"What are you doing?" she shouted.

"I'm doing the puzzle," he said. "I think I've almost got it."

Of course! Zak was a good reader, better than she was, even though he was younger. Thank goodness for Zak! She got down on the floor next to him.

"What can I do to help?" she asked.

"Just pass me the letters," he said. He looked up at the candle. "Fast!"

Mia worked quickly. She passed Zak the letters so that he could make the words spell out Redbeard's message.

The candle continued to burn, wax dripped. The skull tower started to shake and crack. Soon it would cave in.

The candle was almost gone. Mia felt the ground moving. The whole tower was going to collapse.

"Quick, Zak!" she cried. "We're almost out of time!"

She passed him another letter. The candle was almost out and two words were still missing.

The candle started to flicker. Zak made another word. One more to go.

The candle's flame was dying. Mia snatched up the last letters and placed them down. Had she spelled the last word right? There was no time to change it now. She read the message.

United we stand. Divided we fall.

The candle was down to the smallest spark. The tower was shaking. The roof was starting to fall in. This was it!

Mia threw her arms around Zak, and held him tight.

The candle went out. Time was up! With a terrible crash the tower collapsed. The floor split open and Zak and Mia fell through.

CHAPTER 9

PLAY AGAIN?

Mia was lying on Zak's bed with her arms around her little brother. Zak was holding the Z Box. His thumbs were on the controls. He was staring at the screen.

"Look," he said in a very soft voice.

Mia looked. There was a message on the screen.

"Well played! You live to fight another day. Ready to play again?"

Mia shivered.

"I don't like that game," Zak said. "I never want to play it again."

Mia shook her head. "Me neither."

"It's lucky we got that message right," said Zak.

Mia nodded. What if they hadn't? she thought. Where would they be now?

"You did a really good job with that puzzle," Mia said.

"You were great coming to rescue me," said Zak.

Mia grinned. "We were a pretty good team, weren't we?"

"Yeah, we were." Zak grinned too.

He looked down at his feet. He only had one shoe on and they both could guess where the other one was.

"Don't worry. I'll think of something to tell Mom," Mia said.

It had been ages since they'd talked like this, not shouting or arguing. Mia didn't know why. Maybe she should try to be nicer. Maybe Zak wasn't such a little pest after all. Well, not all the time. She thought about him in the tower with that puzzle. He had been good.

There was a loud banging outside. It was garbage day. Mia had an idea. She switched off the Z Box and took out the strange game. "Come on," she said.

Mia and Zak went downstairs and out through the front door into the street.

The garbage truck was right outside their house now. Mia went around the back and threw the game into the truck.

"There, that's the end of that game," she said, rubbing her hands clean.

"Thank goodness," Zak added. He gave Mia a high five.

"Want to play some cards?" Mia asked.

"Yeah," said Zak. He grinned. "But you know I'll beat you."

"We'll see," Mia said with a laugh.

The driver of the garbage truck watched the children in his mirror. He smiled and his eyes seemed to gleam. His cone of white hair shined in the sunlight as he drove away down the street and then vanished.

ABOUT THE AUTHOR

Alan Durant lives and works in England. He has written more than 60 books for kids of all ages — from picture books to teenage thrillers. He also writes many different types of stories, including science fiction, adventure, comedy, and mystery.

Durant wrote the *Gamer* books for his son Kit, but don't think he didn't have any fun. To research the book, Durant spent lots of hours playing video games. He also enjoyed working with his friend, illustrator Sue Mason.

ABOUT THE ILLUSTRATOR

Sue Mason has been a freelance illustrator for five years but has worked in publishing for more than 10 years. Today, Mason illustrates a variety of children's books. She loves creating quirky creatures, especially robots, for both big and little kids. She currently lives and works in London, England.

GLOSSARY

cone (KOHN)—a shape that is round at one end and pointed at the other, such as an ice-cream cone.

damage (DAM-ij)—to harm or hurt something

dodge (DOJ)—to move out of the way of something by moving quickly

drawbridge (DRAW-brij)—a bridge that can be raised or lowered to let people in a building or keep people out

experience (ek-SPEER-ee-uhnss)—something that happens in a person's life

scalp (SKALP)—skin on a person's head

skull and crossbones (SKUHL AND KRAWSS-bohnz)—an image of a human skull over two crossed bones; usually a warning of danger

slot (SLOT)—a long, narrow opening

squawk (SKWOK)—a loud, harsh cry

tentacle (TEN-tuh-kuhl)—long, flexible limbs used by some animals for feeling or grasping. Octopuses have eight tentacles.

DISCUSSION QUESTIONS

1. A mysterious old man with a white cone of hair appears at the beginning and end of the story. Do you think he knows about the video game's power? Why or why not.

2. Do you think Mia could have survived the game without her little brother, Zak? Name at least one skill for each character, which helped them complete the game.

3. At the end of the story, Mia throws away the video game. Would you have made the same decision? Explain your answer.

WRITING PROMPTS

1. What's your favorite video game or television show? Imagine you could jump inside your TV and become the main character. Describe your adventures.

2. On each level of the game, Mia faces a challenge. Pretend you are the author and create a whole new level of the game for Mia to play. What challenges or creatures will she face in your level? Will she succeed?

3. The author gives only a little information about the mysterious old man. Using your imagination, write more about this character. What is his name? Where did he come from? What does he know about the mystery game?

INTERNET SITES

Do you want to know more about subjects related to this book? Or are you interested in learning about other topics? Then check out FactHound, a fun, easy way to find Internet sites.

Our investigative staff has already sniffed out great sites for you!

Here's how to use FactHound:

1. Visit *www.facthound.com*

2. Select your grade level.

3. To learn more about subjects related to this book, type in the book's ISBN number: **1598898736**.

4. Click the **Fetch It** button.

FactHound will fetch the best Internet sites for you!